The Lucky Duck

by Sarah Durkee
illustrated by Dave Prebenna

Between the Lions is a co-production of WGBH Boston and Sirius Thinking, Ltd. *Between the Lions* is funded in part by a grant from the United States Department of Education through the Corporation for Public Broadcasting. Major support is also provided by the Carnegie Corporation of New York, the Park Foundation, The Arthur Vining Davis Foundations, the Charles H. Revson Foundation, and the Institute for Civil Society. National corporate sponsorship is provided by Cheerios® and eToys®.

Library of Congress Cataloging-in-Publication Data
Durkee, Sarah.
The lucky duck / by Sarah Durkee ; illustrated by David Prebenna.
     p. cm.
Summary: Lions in a library turn to various books for ideas to help the title character of "The Lucky, Lucky, Lucky Duck" overcome his irresistible cuteness.
ISBN 0-307-16502-7 — ISBN 0-307-36502-6 (GB)
[1. Ducks—Fiction. 2. Lions—Fiction. 3. Books and reading—Fiction. 4. Characters in literature—Fiction. 5. Libraries—Fiction. 6. Self-perception—Fiction.] I. Prebenna, David, ill. II. Title.

PZ7.D934247 Lu 2000
[E]—dc21   99-87425

A GOLDEN BOOK · New York
Golden Books Publishing Company, Inc. New York, New York 10106

ISBN: 0-307-16502-7 (hardcover)
ISBN: 0-307-36502-6 (GB)   A MM

"It is time to pick new books
for the library," Cleo said.
"This one looks good!" said Lionel.
He held up *The World's Largest Cheese.*

"How about this one?" Cleo asked.
"The Lucky, Lucky, Lucky Duck."
"It looks so cute!" Leona said.
"I love cute duck books!"

The Lucky,
ucky,
Ky
Duck
by Ernestine Darling

"Ick," said Lionel.
"Cute is for babies."
"Let's read it," Theo said.
"Then we can decide."

Theo opened the book.
He read it out loud.

The cute little duck jumps
in a cute little puddle.
Oh, what a lucky duck!

The Lucky,
Lucky,
Lucky
Duck

by Ernestine Darling

The cute little duck splashes in the cute little puddle. Oh, what a lucky, lucky duck!

The cute little duck jumps
out of the cute little puddle
and takes a nap in the sun.
Oh, what a lucky, lucky,
lucky duck!

"Stop!" said Lionel.
"It's too cute!
I can't take it anymore!"

"*You* can't take it anymore?"
  said the Lucky Duck.
"How do you think *I* feel?"
  And right before the lions' eyes,
  the Lucky Duck ripped himself
  out of the book!

The Lucky Duck was very, very mad.

The lions looked at the little duck.
"Awww," they said.
"You are so CUTE!"

The Lucky Duck started to cry.
"I am sick of being cute!" he said.
"Please help me."

"I will help you," Lionel said.
"The library is full of books.
 I'm sure we can find
 a good idea in one of them."
"Thanks," said the duck.

Lionel found a book about dinosaurs.
"Dinosaurs are not cute," said Lionel.
"They are large.
   Maybe you can be large, too."

BIG
DINO
BOOK

They went to ask Heath for help.
Heath was the only dinosaur they knew.

"Can you teach him to be large?"
 Lionel asked Heath.
"Ah!" said Heath proudly.
"You mean huge! Giant! King size!"
"Yes!" said the Lucky Duck.

"Sorry," said Heath.
"I was born large
 like you were born little and cute."
"I do not want to be cute!" said the duck.

Lionel found another book.
This one was about monsters.
"Monsters are not cute," said Lionel.
"Monsters are scary."

Lionel tried to make
the Lucky Duck scary.
He wrapped the duck up
like a mummy.

In walked Leona.
"Boo!" the duck squeaked.

"Awww," said Leona.
"You are so CUTE!"
"Oh, no!" the duck said.
"I do not want to be cute!"

Lionel had another idea.
He grabbed a book called
The Big Bad Wolf!
"Come on!" he said
to the Lucky Duck.

A little later,
Lionel and the Lucky Duck were back.
"Here he is," Lionel said.
"The Big Bad Duck!"

"He's mean," Lionel said.
"He's bad. . . ."

"Awww," everyone said.
"He is so CUTE!"

"Am I doomed
  to be cute forever?"
  cried the duck.
"Why? Why?"

Lionel's face lit up.
"Y!" he said.
"That's the answer!"
He ran off.

When Lionel came back,
he had a new book.
"I changed the L in Lucky to a Y,"
he said proudly.
"My new book is called
The Yucky, Yucky, Yucky Duck."

The Yucky,
Yucky,
Yucky
Duck

by Lionel The Lion

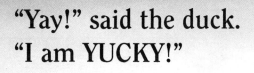

"Yay!" said the duck.
"I am YUCKY!"

Lionel read the book out loud.

The cute little duck jumps
in a cute little mud puddle.
Oh, what a yucky duck!

The Yucky,
Yucky,
Yucky
Duck
by Lionel The Lion

The cute little duck splashes
in the cute little mud puddle.
Oh, what a yucky, yucky duck!

The cute little duck jumps
out of the cute little mud puddle
and takes a nap in the sun.
Oh, what a yucky, yucky,
yucky duck!

The duck loved the Yucky Duck book.
But Leona was a little sad.
"I like the book
where he is LUCKY," she said.

"Well, I like the book
  where he is YUCKY," said Lionel.
"Lucky!" said Leona.
"Yucky!" said Lionel.

Cleo held up her paws.
"We can have both books
in the library," she said.

Lionel and Leona and
the Lucky, Yucky Duck smiled.

And they all lived luckily—
and yuckily—ever after.